Karen's Magic Garden

**Look for these
and other books about Karen
in the
Baby-sitters Little Sister series:**

Little Sister

Karen's Magic Garden
Ann M. Martin

Illustrations by Susan Tang

A
LITTLE APPLE
PAPERBACK

SCHOLASTIC INC.
New York Toronto London Auckland Sydney

ISBN 0-590-69184-8

12 11 10 9 8 7 6 5 4 3 2 1   6 7 8 9/9 0 1/0

Printed in the U.S.A.   40

First Scholastic printing, August 1996

*The author gratefully acknowledges
Gabrielle Charbonnet
for her help
with this book.*

Karen's Magic Garden

Emily Junior

"Okey-dokey, Emily Junior," I said. I picked up Emily Junior and put her down on the floor of my room. She looked at me. She wiggled her nose. Then she scurried over to my bookcase.

"No eating books," I called. Once Emily Junior had nibbled one of my books. That is because she is a rat. I know what you are thinking: Ew. But Emily Junior is not just any old ratty rat. She is my special pet rat. She is so special that I named her after my little sister, Emily Michelle.

It was Wednesday. Which meant it was time to clean Emily Junior's cage. This is what I have to do whenever I clean her cage:

1. Take out Emily Junior. (Well, first I have to shut my bedroom door.)
2. Take out her water bottle. (I refill it every day.)
3. Take out her play wheel.
4. Scoop out all the old cedar shavings and throw them away.
5. Wipe her cage with paper towels.
6. Put in clean cedar shavings, and the water bottle, and the play wheel.
7. Put Emily Junior back in. (And fasten the lid on tight.)

You can see what a hard job it is. But I have to do it. I am Emily Junior's adopted mother.

My name is Karen Brewer. I am seven years old. I have long blonde hair, blue eyes, and some freckles. Since it is August,

I have more freckles than usual.

"Okay, Emily Junior," I called finally. "You have a nice clean cage." I waited a moment. "You are welcome," I said.

Then I heard Mommy calling me.

"Karen!" she called. "Please come to dinner."

"Oh boy!" I jumped up. I was gigundoly hungry. I was looking forward to dinner here at the little house.

(I live at two different houses. A big house and a little house. I know you are wondering why. I will explain that in a minute.)

At the little house live Mommy, Seth, who is my stepfather, Andrew, who is my little brother (he is four going on five), and I. Those are the people. The animals are Rocky, who is Seth's cat, and Midgie, who is Seth's dog, and Bob, who is Andrew's pet hermit crab, and Emily Junior, who you know.

I didn't know it yet, but I was about to get a big surprise.

The Big Surprise

"Pass the potatoes," I said. We were having mashed potatoes. They are my favorite kind of potato. (Except for french fries.)

"What's the magic word?" Mommy asked.

I smiled. "Pleeaaase." Mommy passed the bowl of mashed potatoes. "Please" is not a really, truly magic word. She just meant if I used it, I would get what I wanted. I took some potatoes and passed the bowl to Andrew.

"It is nice to have you here again," Seth

said. He smiled at Andrew and me.

"Thank you," I said. I patted my mashed potatoes into a smooth flat mound. That is not really playing with my food. That is just how I like to eat them. "It is nice to be here."

You are probably wondering where I had been. I will tell you: I had been at the big house.

A very long time ago, when I was little, I lived in only one house — the big one. I lived there with Mommy, Daddy, and Andrew. Then Mommy and Daddy decided that even though they loved Andrew and me very much, they did not love each other anymore. So they got divorced. Mommy and Andrew and I moved to the little house. Daddy stayed in the big house. (It is where he grew up.)

Then Mommy met Seth, and they got married. That is how Seth became my stepfather.

And Daddy met Elizabeth, and *they* got married. So Elizabeth is my stepmother.

And now Andrew and I stay for a month at the big house and a month at the little house.

Now here is the tricky part: At the big house are Daddy, Elizabeth, and Elizabeth's four kids. (Elizabeth was married once before.) Kristy is thirteen, and she is my favorite big stepsister. Sam and Charlie are very old. They go to high school. David Michael is seven like me, but an older seven. Then there is Emily Michelle, who is my favorite little adopted sister. She is two and a half. (Remember, I named Emily Junior after her.) Daddy and Elizabeth adopted her from Vietnam. That is a country that is very far away. After that, Elizabeth's mother, Nannie, came to live at the big house, too. She helps take care of everyone. (Including me.)

So that is a lot of people. There are also Shannon, who is David Michael's puppy, and Boo-Boo, who is Daddy's cat. Boo-Boo is cranky. I stay out of his way. I keep Emily Junior out of his way, too. (Emily Junior goes back and forth with me. And so does Bob.) And I haven't even told you about Crystal Light the Second and Goldfishie. They are our pet dinosaurs. No, they are goldfish!

"Seth and I have some news to share," Mommy said. "Now that you are here, I can tell you both."

Andrew and I looked at each other. I did not know whether to feel scared or excited. I decided to feel excited.

"What? What? What?" I cried. I was bouncing in my chair.

"Indoor voice, Karen," Mommy said.

"What? What? What?" I whispered loudly.

"My family is having a reunion," Mommy said. "It will be the very first Packett family reunion. It will be way up in Lobster Cove, Maine, in about two and a half weeks. And we are going to go. It will be like a little vacation."

I was so surprised that I thought my eyes were going to pop out of my head.

"Oh, boy!" I said, trying to use my indoor voice. "Oh boy, oh boy, oh boy!"

A family reunion! I had never been to one. I love doing new things. And I would meet lots of Mommy's relatives. I bet there would be a million cousins for me to play with. I just knew this was going to be the most gigundoly fabulous vacation ever. There was just one thing:

"Where is Maine?" I asked.

On the Road to Maine

In case you do not know, Maine is way up high on the East Coast of the United States. It is above Stoneybrook, Connecticut, which is where I live. It is above Massachusetts. It is above Vermont and New Hampshire. It is so far north that if you miss Maine and keep going, you will be in Canada. Really. I am not making that up.

Mommy lived in Lobster Cove when she was little. But she had not gone back there in a long time. So she was excited also. And Seth wanted to see some people there who make furniture. (He makes furniture, too. Out of wood.)

Everyone in the little house was as excited as they could be. Especially me.

"Karen, did you pack Goosie?" Mommy asked.

It was two weeks later. We were loading the car to go to Lobster Cove. It was so early in the morning that it was still dark and cool outside. I was sitting on the front steps. I did not feel one bit sleepy. I was so ready to go that I was having a hard time keeping out of Mommy's way. Finally she asked me to sit on the front steps. So I did. But I could not help wiggling and bouncing where I sat.

"Karen?" Mommy repeated as she walked past me.

"Yes," I said. "I have Goosie right here." I held Goosie up so Mommy could see her. Goosie is my little-house stuffed cat. Moosie is my big-house stuffed cat. I forgot to tell you that I have a special name for Andrew and me. I call us Andrew Two-Two and Karen Two-Two. I call us that because we have two of so many things. Two houses, two mommies, two daddies, two families. I even wear two different pairs of glasses. I wear blue ones to read with, and pink ones the rest of the time. I have two of lots of things, one at each house. I even have two best friends. Hannie Papadakis lives across the street and one house down from the big house. Nancy Dawes lives next door to the little house. And I have Goosie and Moosie. Having two of everything makes it easier to move back and forth every month.

Andrew came out of the house and sat down next to me. He looked very tired. "Do you think Bob will be okay?" he asked.

"Yes," I said. "Jessi will take good care of him." Jessi Ramsey is a friend of Kristy's. She was going to take care of our pets while we were away.

While Andrew and I sat there, Mommy and Seth loaded Mommy's car. This is what we packed:

1. One suitcase for Mommy
2. One suitcase for Seth
3. One suitcase for me
4. One suitcase for Andrew
5. One ice chest with drinks and sand-wiches and snacks
6. One box of tapes to listen to
7. One fun bag for me
8. One fun bag for Andrew

You can see why it took a long time to load the car. But at last we were ready. Mommy locked the front door of the house. Andrew and I scrambled into the back seat of the car. We fastened our seat belts. Mommy sat in the front seat next to Seth and fastened her seat belt. Seth started the car and backed out of the driveway. The sky was just barely turning pink. We were on our way to Lobster Cove.

If you have never driven from Stoney-brook, Connecticut, to Lobster Cove,

Maine, you might not know that it takes a very long time. It does.

After I waved good-bye to everything in Stoneybrook, I opened my fun bag. Inside were car games, coloring books, markers, a new book to read, and a brochure. The brochure told me about Maine.

We were on the highway when the sun came up. We passed through two other towns. Seth turned on the air conditioner.

I colored for awhile. I listened to tapes. I read until my head hurt. Andrew and I played three games of checkers. (I let him win once, but he could not tell.) I looked out the window.

"Where are we?" I asked.

"We are almost halfway through Massachusetts," Seth told me.

"Who will be at the reunion, Mommy?" She had already told me, but I wanted to hear it again.

"Aunt Ellen and Uncle Mark," Mommy said. Aunt Ellen is Mommy's sister. I met her once a very long time ago. But I do not remember her. I was only six months old.

"And their daughter, Diana, who is seven, just like you," Mommy went on. "And their other daughter, Kelsey, who is four, like you, Andrew. And my aunt Carol and uncle John, who own the house we are going to. And my cousins Michael and Denise and Mimi and Alison and Richard and Philip. And all their husbands and wives and children. And all of my father's cousins and their wives and husbands and their children. About seventy people in all."

"Will there be many kids there? Besides Diana and Kelsey?" I asked.

Mommy nodded. "Yes. I think there will be quite a few children there."

"Goody," I said. "Is it a big house?" I had already asked this, too. We were going to Maine four days before the reunion started, to visit all our relatives. We would stay with Mommy's aunt Carol and uncle John.

"Yes," Mommy said. "It is a very big house. And there is a very big yard to play in. You will love it."

"I know," I said.

I colored again and read again. Finally I was very, very tired of being in the car. I wanted our vacation to start.

"Are we there yet?" I asked. Mommy had told me not to ask that. But I could not help it.

Seth chuckled in the front seat. Mommy sighed. She said, "Not yet, Karen. We won't be there until dinnertime."

Well, boo and bullfrogs. All this driving was wearing me out. I decided to take a nap.

Still On the Road
to Maine

"Karen, wake up. It's lunchtime."

Mommy was gently patting my shoulder. My eyes blinked open. What did I see? My favorite fast-food restaurant! Yea!

Eating lunch there was a special treat. Andrew got a cool pencil eraser in his *Junior Meal*. I got a small ruler with a hologram on it. After we ate we played on the playground for twenty minutes. Then Mommy said, "Time to go."

To tell you the truth, I did not want to get back in the car. I had been in the car all morning. It is very hard for me to sit still that long and to keep using my indoor voice. (Being inside a car counts as inside, too.) But how else could I get to Lobster Cove?

Andrew and I took turns with his eraser and my ruler. We sang songs. Mommy and Seth sang, too. Mommy sang "Que Sera, Sera," which is one of my favorite songs. We played twenty questions. Seth is very, very good at twenty questions. I am good sometimes. Andrew is usually not very good.

The scenery was soooo pretty. We left Massachusetts. Then we were in New Hampshire — Maine was next. There were many hills. It was fun to go up and down them. The hills were covered with green trees. Mommy said they were maples and pines and firs and oaks.

But still I got bored with being in the car. I will tell you a secret: I whined. I could not help it. Finally we stopped and had a snack at a neato place called the Lighthouse. It looked like a real lighthouse. Mommy bought Andrew and me each a big seashell filled with saltwater taffies. They do not taste salty at all. Then we ran around on the grass for awhile.

I was panting when I got back to the car. My tongue was hanging out. Like a dog.

Mommy smiled at me and smoothed my hair. "Feel better?"

I nodded.

Being in the car made me very tired. I decided to rest my eyes. The next thing I knew, Mommy was saying, "Here we are in Maine! It won't be too much longer now."

Andrew blinked. He had been sleeping too.

"Look — there is the ocean," Seth said, pointing out the window on Mommy's side.

We were on a road smaller than the highway. On one side was nothing but trees,

trees, trees. On the other side was water, water, water. I squinted, but I could not see the end of the water.

"Maine does not look that different from Connecticut," I said. "Except there are more trees."

"Yes," said Mommy. "There are fewer people in Maine and more trees."

I looked out my window. On the ocean were many tiny white boats. Some had sails and some had engines. There were big boats with nets rolled up on the sides.

"Those are fishing boats," Mommy said. "And there is a lobster boat."

"It has cages on it," Andrew said.

"Do I like lobster?" I asked Mommy.

"I do not know," Mommy said. "You can try it and decide."

At dinnertime we stopped at the Friendship House. That is a restaurant. I had spaghetti with meatballs. Andrew had another hamburger. Mommy and Seth had clam chowder and fried fish and french fries. I shared some of Mommy's french fries.

Then guess what we did? You guessed right. We got back in the car. I wanted to yell, Boo and bullfrogs! But I did not.

Soon I saw a sign: Lobster Cove.

"Yea!" I cried.

Lobster Cove

Seth drove through the town and up a hill on the other side. Finally he pulled into a long driveway and parked next to four other cars. The sun was starting to go down.

I looked around. "Where are we? Where is Great-aunt Carol and Great-uncle John's house?"

Mommy pointed. "Right up there."

I saw steps leading up a small hill. They were made of stone. The hill was covered with huge rocks and trees.

"Let's leave the luggage until later," Mommy said.

I felt like a billy goat climbing those stone steps. There was a metal handrail, but I did not use it. I bounced up one step after another.

"Be careful, Karen," Mommy said.

At the top of the steps was a lawn and some trees and the house. It was almost dark, so I could not see the house very well. But I could tell one thing: It was huge.

"Wow," said Andrew.

In front of the house was the ocean. You had to cross some rocks and sand to get to it. In back of the house were bushes and trees and woods.

The side door opened. A nice-looking woman came out, wiping her hands on an apron.

"Hi, Aunt Carol!" Mommy said. "We finally made it!"

There was a lot of hugging after that. Mommy's parents, Grandma and Grandpa Packett, were there. I was glad to see them again. I had not seen them since they moved to Maine.

I met so many new people I practically got dizzy. I kept smiling and saying hello. Everyone hugged Andrew and me. Besides us, almost twenty of Mommy's relatives were staying at the big house.

I liked Aunt Ellen, Mommy's sister, right away. She had hair and eyes like Mommy's, but different.

"And here are my daughters," Aunt Ellen said, putting her arm around two girls. "Diana is seven, and Kelsey is four."

"Just like us," Andrew said.

I looked at Diana. Diana looked at me. Then we smiled at exactly the same time. We looked alike! Not like twins. But more alike than Hannie and I do. Or Nancy and I. This is how we looked alike: Diana had long blonde hair. She had blue eyes. She even had freckles. And we were both wearing woven friendship bracelets. This is how we looked different: Diana was a little taller. She did not wear glasses. I had more freckles.

Kelsey looked at Andrew. "Want to see my frog?" she asked. "His name is Prince Caliber."

"Cool," said Andrew. They ran off.

"Come on. I will show you where we are going to sleep," Diana said.

The grown-ups all had beds upstairs. But guess where the kids were going to sleep.

You will never guess, so I will tell you. On a wide screened-in porch. It had wicker furniture, and a swing hanging from the ceiling. And there was a big pile of sleeping bags.

"See?" said Diana. "It will be great. We can listen to the ocean all night. Let's put our sleeping bags right next to each other."

I grinned. I liked Diana a lot. "We can whisper to each other in the dark."

"We can tell stories," Diana said. "Secret stories."

I thought I had been very tired earlier. But now I felt wide awake. I hugged myself and wiggled with excitement. This was going to be the best family reunion ever!

Cousin Diana

I thought I would never fall asleep that night. Diana and I whispered to each other. We told jokes. We giggled. We listened to the ocean waves. They crashed on the beach again and again.

Then I opened my eyes. It was morning. And I was in Lobster Cove, having a family reunion. When I looked at Diana, she opened her eyes. We grinned.

"Come on!" she said, jumping up. "Last one in line for breakfast is a rotten egg!"

See? That is what I liked about Diana.

She probably had a hard time remembering to use her indoor voice.

We hopped over the kids who were still asleep. Besides me and Diana and Andrew and Kelsey, there were six other cousins. Not to mention two babies who had slept inside. But Diana and I were the only ones who were seven. Besides us, there were:

1. Theresa and Edward and Jonathan. They were all twelve. Theresa and Edward are twins.
2. Henry. He was eleven. He is called Little Henry.
3. Sarah, who was ten.
4. Jennifer, who was five.

More cousins were coming on Sunday. But today was only Thursday.

For breakfast we had corn muffins, bacon, fruit salad, and scrambled eggs. I was starving.

"Mommy," I said while we ate. "Diana and I want to explore the yard. Okay?"

"Okay," she said. She held up three fingers. "Three rules."

"What are they?" I asked.

"One: Do not go near the water unless a grown-up is with you. Two: Do not go on the road or off the property. Three: Stay together so you do not get lost."

"Okay," I said.

"Okay," Diana said.

Are you wondering why Mommy said that about getting lost? I will tell you. Great-aunt Carol and Great-uncle John had a gigundo yard. Big enough to get lost in.

"Let's go!" I said to Diana. She wiped her mouth with her napkin and shoved back her chair.

"Excuse me," she said. Then we ran out the kitchen door and into the backyard.

Well, I do not think I have ever been in such a big backyard. First there was a lawn. Huge bushes with hot-pink flowers surrounded the lawn. At one end was a small metal arch. A rosebush was growing over the arch. There were no roses. It made a little doorway. We went through it.

"Let's pretend we are fairy princesses," I said to Diana. "And we live in the garden. It is our job to keep the garden nice."

"Yeah!" said Diana. "We have to paint flowers different colors and be nice to honeybees. We wear leaf dresses and flowers in our hair."

I grinned. Pretend games are very, very fun if you play them with the right person.

"We have to have flower names," I said. "I will be Princess Violet."

"I will be Princess Rose," said Diana.

As soon as she said that, I wished I were Princess Rose. But it was too late. "Hey, look at this," I said.

We were in a garden closed in by tall hedges. The garden was square, but the plant beds were different shapes and sizes. There were narrow paths. Some of the plants had labels.

"Look at these vegetables," said Diana. "Great-aunt Carol uses them to cook with. Here are some carrots."

We walked through the garden, looking at the different vegetables. I saw cherry tomatoes and bell peppers and lettuce and cabbage. (Ugh.) The sun was making my hair hot.

"I am thirsty, Princess Violet," Diana said. "Let's get something to drink before I shrivel up."

"Me, too, Princess Rose!" I said. We ran back through the arch and across the yard and into the kitchen.

We found a big pitcher of lemonade in the kitchen. We each slurped down a glassful.

Diana and I heard people laughing in the living room. The living room was very big. There was a stone fireplace that I could stand inside.

All the grown-ups (and the two babies) were on the floor. Piles of scrapbooks and boxes of photos and papers were spread around them.

"What are you doing?" I asked.

"We are making a family tree," Aunt El-

len said. "We have taped together these long rolls of paper. Now we are writing in all of our names."

"And all of our children's names," said Mommy.

"And all of our parents' names," Aunt Janet said. "And their parents' names."

"As far back as we can go," said Uncle Henry. (Little Henry is named after him.) "This way, we will have a record of our whole family."

"Cool," I said.

"Look, Karen," Mommy said. "Here is our branch of the family tree."

The Princesses Explore

Mommy showed me where she was on the tree. There was her name, Lisa Packett Brewer Engle, and a small picture of her. Then there was Daddy's name. A line led to a blank.

"Fill in your name," Mommy said, handing me a pencil. "We will paste your latest school picture here."

I wrote my name: **KAREN BREWER**. I wrote my birthday next to my name. Then I glued my picture onto an outline of a leaf. Andrew had written: ANDREW. Mommy filled in his birthday and his last name. He glued down a snapshot that Mommy gave him. It showed Andrew sitting on his tricycle.

Another line led to Seth's picture. "Seth Engle," it said.

"Way cool," I said.

Aunt Ellen showed Diana their family branch. Diana wrote her name and glued in her picture. Aunt Ellen had only one husband line. Mommy had two.

"Why aren't there any pictures down there?" I asked. I pointed to the bottom of the tree, by the roots.

"We are still working on that," Great-aunt Carol said. "That is the oldest part of the tree. We hope to fill it in, but it is hard. Some of the people were born over a hundred years ago."

"Wow," said Diana.

"Yeah, wow," I said. "I like our family tree."

After lunch Princess Rose and I were very busy. We explored the rest of the wilderness. We needed to find a safe place for a bunny family to live. They had been kicked out of their old home by a mean witch.

(This is all still just pretend. There were no bunnies and no witch. Back in Stoneybrook there is a real witch, but that is another story.)

The yard was so huge that we did not get to explore all of it.

"Look at this," I called to Princess Rose.

"That is a summer house," Diana said. "Mommy told me about it."

We were in front of a little building. It did not really look like a house. It looked like the bandstand in the park back in Stoneybrook. It was open on all sides, and had steps. Inside were benches. It was a good home base for a couple of fairy princesses.

I stood on a bench and used my magic telescope. "I do not see the bad witch anywhere," I said. "But I do see trees with real, live apples on them."

"We better go explore them, Princess Violet," said Diana. "In case the bunnies want to live there."

There was a whole field of apple trees. The apples were small and green. We could not eat them. They would have made us sick. At the edge of the field was one very old apple tree. It had a branch that grew close to the ground. The branch was just wide enough for two fairy princesses to sit on, side by ·side. We could even bounce a little. With every breath I took, I smelled and tasted apples. I was in heaven.

"This will be our secret sitting place," I said to Diana. "We can sit here and tell each other secrets."

"Yes," Diana said. "And I know a secret right now. We are going out to dinner. All of us. Tonight."

I sat up. I sat up so high that I bumped my head on the branch above me. But I was not hurt. I laughed aloud. I love going out to dinner!

Lobster, Clams, and Bread Pudding

Well, there is nothing more fun than going to dinner with twelve grown-ups and twelve children and two babies.

At the restaurant they pushed six tables together in a long line. Diana and I sat between my mommy and her mommy. There was a basket of crackers in front of us. We ate about a million crackers. For dinner we had the exact same thing: fish sticks and french fries and salad with ranch dressing. We were twins.

Mommy and Seth both ordered lobster.

Mommy gave me a little piece. I thought it was rubbery. Andrew wanted fried clams.

"Are you sure?" Mommy asked.

Andrew nodded hard.

And you know what? He liked them. He ate every one, except one he gave to Mommy and one he gave to me. I did not like it. I ate it very fast. Then I took a big gulp of water. Then I ate a french fry to give my mouth a new taste. Diana and Andrew and Kelsey and I all had bread pudding for dessert. When I was little I thought bread pudding sounded gross. But now I know it is very delicious. Unlike clams.

Our restaurant was at the marina. We could sit and look out the window at the boats. The sun was setting and it made their sails turn pink. I decided Maine was just as pretty as Connecticut.

By the time the grown-ups had finished their coffee, I was very tired. I was worn out from exploring all day. It is not easy being a fairy princess. Mommy was holding Andrew. I crawled into Seth's lap. I leaned against his shoulder. I rested my eyes.

I thought about Diana, and breakfast, and the family tree. I thought about vegetables, and the apple trees, and about lunch. I thought about the woods and the summer house that we had found. I thought about dinner and bread pudding. It had been a gigundoly perfect day, I decided. Tomorrow would be perfect, too.

Exploring the Attic

"Ugh!" I said as I opened my eyes on Friday morning. "This is not a perfect way to wake up."

I was in my sleeping bag. I did not want to get up. It was cold outside.

"Yuck," Diana said. Only her eyes and her nose were peeking out of her sleeping bag. "Double yuck."

Rain was pattering on the roof of our porch. Rain was splashing through the screens. Rain was running down the gutters. Rain was dripping off of every leaf of every tree. So much for another perfect day.

Just then Great-aunt Carol came to the door of our porch.

"Up and at 'em, kids!" she cried cheerfully. "Homemade doughnuts and applesauce for breakfast."

Diana's face poked out of her sleeping bag.

I came out up to my shoulders.

We looked at each other. "Let's go!" I yelled. We threw off our sleeping bags and raced inside.

"Now what?" Little Henry grumbled. It was after breakfast. We were sitting by the fireplace in the living room. The fire was crackling and hissing. I liked being toasty by the fire. But it was not as good as being outside.

Some of the grown-ups were working on the family tree again. Some were doing a jigsaw puzzle. (It was too hard for me.)

Some were in the kitchen. They were starting to bake and cook for the reunion on Sunday.

"I wish we could go exploring," I said to Diana.

"Me, too," she said.

"I have an idea," Little Henry said. "Let's explore the house."

I thought that was a very good idea.

"Yes," said Diana. "And while we are exploring, we could look for my bracelet. The one with hearts on it. I cannot find it."

"Okay. I am the head archaeologist," Theresa said. "We must explore this ruin. I say we start with the attic."

I did not think we would find Diana's bracelet in the attic, but it sounded fun anyway.

We went up to the third floor. We found five small storage rooms and three more guest bedrooms, but no door to the attic.

"So far this exploring is not very exciting," Diana said to me.

I nodded. There was only one more door

to open. I opened it. "I found it!" I cried.
"I found the attic!"

My cousins crowded around. There was
a dark staircase, leading up.

Theresa said, "Since I am the head archaeologist, I should go first." She did not
look sure about this. But we all nodded.

Theresa crept up the dark, dusty staircase. We crept up after her.

Jonathan found a light switch and turned
it on.

"Oooh," I said.

"Ahhh," said Diana.

The attic was huge, and full of all kinds
of stuff.

"*This* is what I call exploring," I said happily.

"Look over here!" Jennifer cried. "This
trunk is full of old-fashioned clothes."

"Let's try them on," said Sarah.

"I found a box of toys," Jonathan said.
He pulled out a small wooden horse. Andrew, Sarah, and Kelsey ran to the box.

"Wow! This is so cool," Edward said.

"An ancient telescope. Let's see if it works."

Diana and I looked at each other. We did not know what to do first. Should we try on clothes? Look through the telescope? Check out the toys? Then, far back under the roof, I saw a small, dark, dusty trunk. That was for us.

Diana helped me pull it out. I blew some dust off of it. On the front of the trunk were two letters: *A* and *D*. It was not locked.

"Talk about cool," I said.

Inside the lid of the trunk was a name and a date: Annemarie Dillon — 1892.

"That was one of the names in the roots of our family tree," Diana said.

"These must be Annemarie's things." I pulled out a doll. Inside the trunk was a small wooden box with doll clothes. And a photo album with a leather cover. It said "Memories" on it in gold ink.

"This is a whole book of photographs," Diana said. "I bet Mommy would like some for the family tree."

"I bet you are right," I agreed. "Here are some other books, too. They are filled with writing. Let's take everything downstairs."

"Good idea. It is very dusty up here," Diana said.

"I know just where we can go," I said.

The Secret Diaries

"You are right," Diana said. "This is perfect."

We sat on the windowseat in the library. Rain dripped down the windows. But now I did not mind so much.

Diana opened the photo album. "These people are all wearing funny clothes."

"It is very old," I said. "These three little books are diaries. Annemarie Dillon wrote them during the summer of eighteen ninety-two."

"Wow," said Diana, peering over my

shoulder. "What do they say?"

"It is hard to read," I said. "But I will try."

I read out loud:

"June second, eighteen ninety-two

"Dear Diary,

"My name is Annemarie Eugenia Dillon. I am nine years old. This summer, my parents and I are vacationing with my grandparents in Lobster Cove, Maine."

I could not believe it. Annemarie Dillon had come to stay in this very house, over a hundred years ago!

"This is so cool," Diana whispered.

"I know," I whispered back. I read some more out loud:

"Tomorrow I will meet my cousin Pauline for the first time. She is nine years old, like me. She is called Polly. I have planned many pleasant things to do together. And I have made her a gift: a pillow filled with rose petals from Grandmother's garden. I have embroidered Polly's name on it. I hope it will make her feel welcome."

"Is the pillow in the trunk?" I asked.

Diana shook her head. "No, I do not think so. You know what? They are just like us. They are cousins. They are the same age. And they had not met before."

I smiled. "That is so neat."

I skipped ahead to the back of the diary. The handwriting was very hard to read sometimes.

"June fourteenth, eighteen ninety-two
"Dear Diary,
"Polly was crying again last night. I wish I could cheer her somehow. But since her mother's death, she has been so very sad. I do not know what to do."

"That is awful," Diana said. "Polly's mother died."

"She was only nine years old," I said.

"June sixteenth, eighteen ninety-two
"Dear Diary,
"I have decided there is only one thing to do for Polly. Although I was sworn to secrecy, I will show Polly the magic garden. Perhaps once she is inside the garden walls and surrounded by its secret beauty, her heart will begin to mend."

"A magic garden!" I cried.
"Shh!" Diana put her finger to her lips. "It was their secret. Now it is our secret, too."

I pretended to zip my mouth shut and throw away the key, to show I could keep a secret. Once I had gotten in trouble because I did not keep a secret. Since then I have been much better at it.

I opened the next book.

"July second, eighteen ninety-two

"Dear Diary,

"Dare I believe that Polly seems less sad? Today, whilst in the magic garden, she seemed almost to smile when a sparrow sang to her. And last night she had no nightmares. I think the garden is working its magic on her, as I knew it would."

"That garden must have been *here*," Diana said, looking out the window. "They were staying in this house."

"But we explored the whole yard," I reminded her. "We did not see any magic garden."

"Maybe it is not here anymore. Or . . . was it the vegetable garden?"

"No." I shook my head. "This magic garden has walls around it. I did not see any walls in the yard."

"Look through the other diaries," Diana said. "Maybe Annemarie says where it is."

I was very excited. A magic garden! Right

here in Lobster Cove! And it would be our secret: mine and Diana's.

"Oh, there you are, girls," said Aunt Ellen. "It is time for lunch now. Wash your hands, okay?"

"Okay," we said. We hid the diaries under a cushion.

"After lunch we will solve the mystery of the magic garden," Diana said.

"The mystery of the magic garden," I repeated. A shiver went down my spine.

Long-Ago Cousins

After lunch the rain stopped. The sun shone brightly. Diana and I took the last diary and ran outside. In the summer-house, we sat on a bench.

I opened the diary and read out loud again:

"August twenty-fifth, eighteen ninety-two
"Dear Diary,
"I can't believe the summer is almost over. Soon Mama and Papa and I must

go home. I do not want to leave Polly. She is my best friend in the whole world. We have done something special. We made 'memory boxes.' In our boxes we placed special mementos of our summer together. Then we hid them in the magic garden. We have vowed to return next year and open the boxes together. Unless we are together, we will not open them."

I looked at Diana. She was bouncing with excitement.

"Memory boxes!" she said. "What a cool idea. It must have been so neat the next summer when they found them and opened them again."

"Yes," I said. "They were very good friends. Like us."

Diana smiled at me. "Come on! Let's use the clues in the diaries to help us find the magic garden."

She took the diary and began turning the pages. "It says the magic garden is past the

54

apple tree with the bent branch," she said.

I read, too. "It is past the vegetable garden and the rose arch."

"It is not so far as the woods," Diana said.

"It is not close to the ocean," I said.

Do you know what? We found the magic garden! It was practically right in front of our eyes! We had walked past it the day before, but had not seen it. It was covered with overgrown bushes and vines and even some small trees.

"This brick wall is not high," said Diana.

"I am sure we could climb over it," I said. I am a very good climber.

And that is what we did. The vines made it easy. At the exact same time, Diana and I scrambled over the wall around the magic garden.

We jumped down.

"Wow," I said.

"Yes, wow," Diana agreed.

"No one has been here for a long time," I said. The magic garden was not big.

56

Rosebushes grew next to the walls. There were pebbled paths that we could hardly see. Overgrown plants, old sticks, leaves, and vines covered everything. Once inside, we could see a metal gate leading out.

"Look," said Diana. "Here is an old stone bench."

We sat on it in the sun. "I bet Annemarie and Polly sat here together, years and years and years ago," I said.

"They called this the magic garden because when they made wishes here, their wishes came true," Diana said. (We had read that in the diary.)

"Let's make wishes ourselves," I said.

Diana and I closed our eyes and made secret wishes.

I smiled at Diana. "I have a great idea," I said. "But we will need a family meeting."

The Magic Garden

"Where should I put this?" Little Henry asked. He was pushing a wheelbarrow full of small rocks.

I pointed. "Over there, where Uncle Mark is making new paths."

"I am going to trim all these vines," Seth said. "Then we can see the brick wall."

"A fountain!" Diana cried. "I found a fountain!"

Back at the house, Diana and I had called a family meeting. We had decided not to keep the magic garden a secret. (But we still kept our wishes secret.) At the family meeting, we told everyone about the garden. We asked for permission to clean it up. That was my brilliant idea: to try to make the garden look like it did when Annemarie and Polly used to go there.

Great-aunt Carol and Great-uncle John gave us permission. Then everyone wanted to join in. All my relatives who weren't baking and cooking for the family reunion decided to help us with the magic garden.

And now here we were.

The sun was shining, but it was not too hot. We were filling garbage bags full of old leaves, bush trimmings, and vines.

I was raking the flower beds. Under the blanket of leaves, I found small green plants trying to push their way through. It was just like in *The Secret Garden* by Frances Hodgson Burnett. That was a very great book that Kristy read to me.

Carefully I cleaned spaces around the plants, so they could breathe. I thought about how no one had taken care of them

for a gigundoly long time. Were the little plants happy that we were here?

We worked in the garden a long, long time.

Finally Diana and I flopped down on the stone bench. (We had found three other benches.)

"This is hard work," Diana said.

"Very hard." I had leaves in my hair. My hands were dirty. I was hot and sweaty.

"My goodness gracious!" said a voice.

Great-aunt Carol was standing at the little metal gate of the garden. (We could use the gate now.)

"This is completely amazing!" she said. "To think I've lived here all these years and never knew about this special garden."

Diana and I sat up proudly.

"It's going to be a beautiful little garden," Aunt Ellen said. "These rosebushes are already setting buds for the fall."

"And I believe there are bulbs beneath the soil," Mommy said. "Next spring you will have crocuses and lily-of-the-valley and tulips."

"I found a birdbath in the old garden shed that I will set up here," Uncle Philip said.

"Many birds and butterflies live here," I added. "They knew about the garden the whole time."

"This is too wonderful," Great-aunt Carol said. "You all deserve a special treat. I will bring a big pitcher of lemonade, and then I have some surprises for you."

The Two Wishes

"I got my wish," I whispered to Diana later.

"You wished for fried chicken?" she asked.

"Nooo!" I laughed. "My wish was to have a picnic on the beach. Mommy told me she used to have them. I wanted to have one, too."

Great-aunt Carol's surprises had been a big, lovely fire on the beach, and a picnic supper. We even went swimming. In case you do not know, the ocean water off the coast of Maine is very, very, very, very cold. Even in August. But we were all so hot and dirty and sweaty that we did not care.

Seth and Uncle Mark and Uncle Philip and Uncle Richard stayed in the water the longest. I lasted two and a half seconds. I ran in very fast, yelled, and ran out again. I did not want to turn into an ice cube! Then I wrapped myself in an old blanket and curled up by the fire. I felt gigundoly fabulous.

Since my wish had come true, I told Diana about it. For our picnic supper we had fried chicken, corn bread, and potato salad.

The sun went down. I felt warm and full and sleepy. I was leaning on Mommy by the fire. Andrew was sleeping in Seth's lap. Kelsey was sleeping in Aunt Ellen's lap. Diana was roasting marshmallows on a stick in the fire. Uncle Mark was helping her.

"I think it is almost time to go to bed, Di," Aunt Ellen said.

"I was thinking the same thing," Mommy said.

I snuggled up to her.

"Oh, I completely forgot," Aunt Ellen said. She reached in her pocket carefully (so she would not wake Kelsey), and pulled out a bracelet with pink hearts on it.

"I found your bracelet, Diana," she said. "It was in my suitcase by mistake."

Diana's eyes were wide. "Thank you, Mommy. I am so glad you found it."

Then Diana ate her marshmallow and moved closer to me. "Karen, my secret wish was to find my heart bracelet," she whispered. "My wish came true! The garden really is magic, just like Annemarie said."

Getting Ready

On Saturday morning my relatives and I worked in the garden again. It was like a miracle.

Now the paths were clear. The flower beds were clean, and summer blooms were showing brightly. The fountain had been cleaned out. Great-uncle John said he would have it repaired and put water in it.

The rosebushes had been trimmed. The brick walls were almost clear of their vines. The garden looked beautiful.

After lunch it began to rain again.

"Boo and bullfrogs," I said. "Great-aunt Carol said I could plant some flowers in the magic garden. Now I cannot."

"I need you inside anyway, Karen," Mommy said. "You and Diana can help get things ready for the reunion tomorrow."

"What should we do?" Diana asked.

"You may decorate cookies," said Aunt Denise.

"You may squeeze lemons for lemonade," said Aunt Ellen.

"You may make name tags for everyone," said Mommy.

Diana and I looked at each other and smiled. Those were fun jobs!

That is how we spent the afternoon. Diana and I decorated a gazillion sugar cookies. We had tubes of frosting, and we drew a big P on each cookie. P for the Packett family. Then we squeezed lemons until our arms hurt. I liked being in the kitchen. It was full of people and noise and running around. No one told me to use my indoor voice. No one told me to stop wiggling.

Then Mommy gave us a box of paper name tags and a long list of names. We wrote names on name tags until our hands felt as if they would fall off. On my tag I wrote "Karen Brewer," and decorated it with violet flowers. Diana's said "Diana Wells," and she drew red roses on it.

In the living room, grown-ups kept working on the family tree. It was almost done. There were a few names missing by the roots, and some pictures, too.

Uncle Mark gave us kids a long roll of paper. We spread it on the floor and made a "Welcome" banner for everyone. I drew butterflies on my section of the banner.

When we were done, Uncle Michael and Aunt Denise hung it on the front porch over the door. It looked beautiful.

There were many things to be done for the reunion. Even when the rain stopped, we still helped. (I wanted to go back to the magic garden. But I did not.) These are the things we did:

1. Gathered tons of flowers to put in vases everywhere.
2. Sorted plastic forks, spoons, and knives.
3. Unwrapped paper plates and plastic cups.
4. Blew up balloons.
5. Swept the front porch.
6. Helped put chairs around the outside tables.

In the late afternoon, Mommy, Seth, Andrew, and I went on an outing. We hiked around the countryside near the house. It was beautiful. Andrew caught a toad. Mommy and Seth picked blueberries. I looked for a bear but I did not see one. All I found were a few bugs.

"Time to go back," said Mommy.

"Okay," said Andrew.

"Okay," I said. Even though I wanted to stay.

But guess what I saw on our way back. Five deer!

For dinner we had take-out Chinese food. We each got a fortune cookie. I love fortune cookies! I cracked mine open and ate half of it. Then I read my fortune. It said: "Happy is the house that shelters a friend."

Just like this great big house. It had sheltered Annemarie and Polly, and now Diana and me.

Well, for heaven's sake.

The Packett
Family Reunion

My face was warm when I woke up on Sunday. I blinked. It was sunny.

"Hooray!" I cried. Too late I remembered that my cousins were asleep. Diana woke up, then Little Henry, then Theresa, then Sarah.

"I am sorry I woke you," I said. "But it is sunny. It is a beautiful day for our family reunion."

Diana smiled at me from her sleeping bag. She did not mind my waking her.

"Hooray!" she yelled. She jumped up so

fast that she almost got tangled in her sleeping bag. Then she grabbed my hands and we danced in a little circle. We tried not to step on anyone. Diana knew exactly how I felt: excited, happy, and bouncy.

"Come on, kids," Aunt Denise called. "We have a lot to do this morning. Roll your sleeping bags neatly and stack them by the wall."

Right after breakfast, carloads of people began to arrive. Diana and I sat on the front steps. We kept jumping up and down and running around the porch.

"Hello!" I called when the first people came. "Hello! Welcome to the Packett family reunion!"

Diana and I were wearing our name tags. Mommy had put us in charge of the nametag table. As our relatives arrived, we helped them find their name tags. They peeled off the backs and stuck them to their clothes.

There were more people than I could count. There were aunts and uncles, mothers and fathers, cousins, teenagers, kids, and babies. And they were all carrying food.

"I cannot wait for lunch," Diana said to me.

"Karen," Mommy said from the porch. "Here are some new cousins: Nicky, Benjamin, Clare, and Laura. Why don't you and Diana show them the magic garden?"

"Yes," I said. "We will be happy to. Everyone, come this way."

My new cousins loved the magic garden. Diana and I took turns telling them how we had found it. (We did not talk too much about the diaries. Those were still our special discovery.)

By noon, all of our relatives had arrived. Great-aunt Carol rang a giant bell.

"Welcome, everyone!" she said. "You've come from all over, near and far, to be with your kinfolk at this first Packett family reunion. There are a lot of warm feelings here today — and a lot of food, too."

Everyone laughed.

"But before we fill our stomachs, let's fill our hearts. Everyone, turn and hug the people to the left and right of you."

This was fun! I hugged Diana on one side, and Uncle Michael on the other.

"Now, John has a memento of this special day," Great-aunt Carol said.

Great-uncle John took something from a box and held it up.

Diana laughed. He had made "PACKETT FAMILY REUNION" T-shirts!

"Who's an extra large?" Great-uncle John asked.

Diana and I decided to get extra larges so that we could use them as sleeping shirts.

After everyone had a T-shirt, it was time to eat.

In the backyard were tables with food and other tables with chairs. It looked like an outdoor restaurant. There were so many things to eat: baked beans, potato salad, coleslaw, corn-on-the-cob, rolls, muffins, fruit salad. There were bowls of chips and pretzels, and platters of hot dogs, hamburgers, and barbecued ribs. *Five* different grills were cooking things.

One table had only desserts: the cookies we had decorated, cakes, pies, caramel apples. And that wasn't all!

On the beach, Seth and Uncle Richard had dug a huge pit and lined it with wet seaweed. Now they were steaming clams, mussels, lobsters, potatoes, and more corn.

I looked at all the food and sighed. "I do not know where to start first," I said.

"I want a hamburger and some chips, then some coleslaw and potato salad," Diana said. "Then maybe a hot dog. Then maybe dessert."

"We will have to go slow if we want to eat everything," I said.

That is what we did. We sat beneath a huge pine tree with our plates of food piled high. First Diana took a bite. Then I took a bite. We would not chew at the same time.

But when I finally finished my last piece of cake with ice cream, I just wanted to lie down.

"The magic garden," Diana moaned.

We got up and sort of rolled ourselves to the magic garden. Diana lay down on one bench. I was on another. We lay on our backs and looked at the sky.

Diana giggled. "I am wishing that my stomach felt better. Do you think I will get my wish?"

"Yes," I said. "Not for awhile, though." I giggled also.

After a long time we both felt better.

"I guess I got my wish," Diana said, sitting up.

"That's because this is a magic garden," I said. I sat up, too.

Then we heard Great-aunt Carol ringing her big bell again.

"Come on, everyone!" she called. "It's time for games!"

"Games?" I asked Diana.

Diana grabbed my hands. "Let's go!"

Family Games

We played Packett Family Reunion games. I was on the blue team. Diana was on the red team. Mommy was on the blue team with me. Seth and Andrew were on the green team. There were eight teams in all.

"Go, Karen, go!" I heard Mommy shout.

I was hopping against Seth, Aunt Ellen, Nicky, Theresa, and Kelsey in the sack race. I pulled my sack up tighter and hopped as fast as I could. Halfway through the race I wished that I had not had that second piece of coconut cake.

Kelsey tripped and fell on her sack. Then Nicky fell. Seth was hopping very hard. But not as hard as I was!

Just as Seth was rounding a bush and hopping toward the finish line, he tripped. Hop, hop, hop. I hopped right past him, and crossed the finish line first! Aunt Ellen was second. Theresa was third.

For my first-place prize I got a small pink plastic purse that was full of wooden beads to make a necklace. Yea!

We played lots of games. There was a relay race, an egg-toss contest, a three-legged race, a frying-pan balancing contest, a pin-the-lobster-on-the-trap game, and many others. We played until it was time for a family photograph.

We all crowded onto the wide porch steps. The littlest kids sat on the bottom steps. The middle kids sat on the middle steps. Then the grown-ups filled the rest of the steps. We were all smushed together

like sardines! I could not stop giggling. Great-uncle John set his camera on a tripod and pressed the timer. Then he ran to the porch and sat next to cousin Jennifer. I remembered to smile big just in time. Click!

"I will have copies made, and send everyone a group portrait," said Great-uncle John.

We all climbed down the steps. It was time to eat again. I only ate a little bit this time.

Then it started to get dark. Everyone began hugging and kissing good-bye. They loaded their cars. I was sad when my relatives drove away. I had met so many new people. And they were my family!

During the day, people had filled in spaces on the family tree. They had brought family records and photographs. Now there was only one photograph missing: Polly's mother.

"We will probably never find one," Great-aunt Carol said. "She lived such a long time ago. And she died very young."

More people left. Uncle Richard and

Aunt Denise left. Theresa and Edward left.

"Good-bye! Good-bye!" I called, waving at their car. "Thank you for helping with the magic garden!"

Aunt Mimi and Uncle Henry left with Little Henry and Jennifer.

"Be sure to write!" I yelled.

Uncle Philip and Aunt Alison left with Jonathan.

"See you at the next family reunion!" I shouted.

Soon everyone was gone except Mommy, Seth, Andrew, me, Great-aunt Carol, Great-uncle John, Aunt Ellen, Uncle Mark, and Kelsey and Diana.

Diana and I sat on the back porch. The grown-ups were gathering trash and putting away leftover food. Diana and I shared one more piece of pie. I felt kind of blue.

The family reunion had been so much fun. Almost *too* fun. Now it was over. The sun had gone down. It was getting chilly. I wondered what was happening back in Stoneybrook. I wondered about Emily Junior and Bob. I rubbed my arms.

"Gee, it is very quiet now," Diana said.

"That is just what I was thinking," I said. I tried to smile. "I think you are connected to my brain."

Diana giggled. "It was fun seeing all the cousins."

"Playing all the games," I added.

"Eating all the food." Diana frowned and put down the pie plate. "Maybe too much food."

"Soon we will be going home."

"You know what?" Diana asked. She did not wait for me to answer. "We still have the magic garden."

"You are right!" I said. I felt a tiny bit less blue. "We can play in it tomorrow."

"You know what else?" Diana asked again. "We could explore the attic again now, just the two of us. Maybe we will find something else."

So that is what we did.

More Secret Diaries

We looked through the telescope. We tried on old clothes. I looked very funny wearing old clothes.

"Look back there," I said. I pointed under the eaves. "I see another old box."

Diana and I pulled it out. It was tied shut with string.

"Look, look!" Diana cried. "There is *AED* written on the side."

"Annemarie Eugenia Dillon!" I was very excited again. I did not feel the tiniest bit blue. Quickly we untied the string.

Guess what we found? More diaries, written by Annemarie.

Diana looked at me. I looked at her.

"To the windowseat," we said at the exact same time.

"These were written in nineteen-oh-two," Diana said, opening a diary. "That is ten years after the first ones."

I counted on my fingers. "Annemarie must have been nineteen years old. Read some out loud."

Diana squinted and turned the diary this way and that. Finally she read out loud:

"June fifth, nineteen-oh-two

"Dear Diary,

"Toby and I have come to Lobster Cove to see my family. I cannot believe that in only five days I will be Toby's bride."

"Bride!" I shrieked.

Diana's eyes were big. "She was only nineteen."

She read some more:

"It is good to be back here — home to so many happy memories. Toby seems to love it as much as I do. I have only one wish: that my whole family were here to share in our joy. But as you know, Polly is still in Europe. Even though I haven't seen her in ten years, my heart misses her."

"Didn't they see each other the next summer?" I asked. "They were supposed to meet here the very next summer."

"Everything is just as I remember it. The roses are in bloom, the ocean air is fresh. I think back to my girlhood days, and miss Polly sorely. If only her father hadn't remarried! If only they still lived in America! Still, at least I have my darling Toby. I plan to show him the 'magic garden' after dinner this evening."

"Oh my gosh," Diana breathed. "Maybe they never saw each other again. Maybe Polly never came back."

"Diana, if Polly and Annemarie did not meet the next summer, maybe they never looked for their memory boxes," I said. I could feel a tingle starting down at my toes. "Maybe the memory boxes are still hidden in the magic garden!"

"We have to look for them!" Diana cried. "We have to look for them before we both go back home!"

"Girls?" Mommy said. She was standing in the doorway. "It is bedtime. Please come take your baths."

I groaned. We would have to wait until the next day to see if the memory boxes were where Annemarie and Polly had left them — way back in 1892.

Long-Ago Memory Boxes

I did not think I would ever want to eat again. But when I woke up on Monday morning, I was starving.

Diana and I ate breakfast very quickly. Then we ran outside with all the early journals — the ones Annemarie had written when she was nine years old.

We sat on a warm stone bench in the magic garden. Diana looked through one book. I looked through another.

"Here it is," I cried. "Here is the section

about the memory boxes." Diana leaned over my shoulder to see.

"Hmm," Diana said. "It says they are hidden in the wall. What wall?"

"She must mean the wall of the magic garden," I said firmly. "But how could that be? The walls are made of bricks."

"We cannot open the walls," Diana agreed. "Unless we had a really big hammer."

I stood up, closed my eyes, and wished a secret wish.

Then we began to look at the garden walls. Were the memory boxes buried next to them? Was there a secret compartment? We tapped the bricks. We looked for clues that would tell us where they were.

But we could not find them. I flopped down on the little patch of grass (neatly mowed and raked) in front of the empty fountain. There were two fountain statues — one on each side. They were women wearing long, flowing robes. They looked very old. Then . . . did I see something? I went closer to them. Yes! By one statue a very small *A* was scratched into the closest brick. There was a little *P* on a brick close to the other statue.

"Diana!" I cried. "Quick, come here!"

Together we scrabbled at the brick with the *A* on it. Holding my breath, I pulled at it as hard as I could.

Finally it came loose in my hands. I was pulling so hard I fell backward.

After that it was easy. The brick next to that one came out right away. Then I carefully stuck my hand in the hole . . . and pulled out an old metal biscuit box.

"Annemarie's memory box," Diana whispered. "After all this time."

My wish had come true. I had wished that we would find the memory boxes. See? It really was a magic garden. I looked up at Diana. "We should not open it yet," I said. "We should find Polly's also. Then open them together."

"Good idea," said Diana.

Well, Polly's box was behind two loose bricks by the *P* on the other side. Diana held Polly's box, and I held Annemarie's. We sat on the grass facing each other.

"One, two, three . . . now!" I cried. We flung open the boxes.

Inside, the boxes were almost exactly alike. These are the things we found:

1. A locket shaped like a heart. (They had pictures inside.)
2. A faded hair ribbon with a real lock of hair. (Annemarie's was blonde, Polly's was dark brown.)
3. A half of a ticket to a county fair.
4. A fancy pencil.
5. A fancy postcard.

Annemarie's box also had a tiny china doll in it. Her clothes were moldy.

"Ew," I said.

Polly's box had a tiny pillow in it. "Polly" was embroidered on it in pink thread.

"Her welcoming pillow!" Diana said. We both sniffed it. It still smelled a little like rose petals.

Also in Polly's box was a photo of a young woman. On the back it said "Mamma Dear."

"The missing family-tree picture!" I said happily. "We have to show this to Great-aunt Carol."

Diana closed Polly's box, and I closed Annemarie's. Then we ran to the big house.

"Everyone, come quick!" I called. "Please," I added. "Diana and I have something very important to tell you."

"And show you," Diana said.

It took us a long time to tell everyone the whole story of Annemarie and Polly and the diaries and the memory boxes. Then we opened them and showed what was inside.

"Well, I declare," said Great-aunt Carol,

picking up the old photograph. "This is the very thing we needed."

Carefully she pasted in the picture of Polly's mother at the bottom of the family tree.

Mommy hugged me. "You girls have been real detectives."

I nodded proudly.

Great-aunt Carol smiled at Diana and me. "You both deserve a special prize, for finding the last, most difficult photograph. Would you like to keep Annemarie's and Polly's memory boxes?"

"Yes!" I cried. "Please."

"Double yes!" Diana said.

We jumped up and down.

Then Mommy looked at me, and I stopped.

I opened my box, took out the locket, and put it on. (Mommy helped me.) Then I opened it. Inside were two faded brown photographs of girls. One had blonde hair, one had dark brown. They were Annemarie and Polly.

Diana put on her locket. The same two pictures were inside.

She looked at me, and I looked at her. Using our special cousin-mind-reading, we each decided to keep them forever.

New Memory Boxes

Later that afternoon, Mommy and Seth took Diana, Kelsey, Andrew, and me to the beach. Most of the beach was just big rocks, little rocks, and rocks in between. But there was also a small strip of sand. That's where the fire had been. And the big cooking pit on Sunday. Now we walked on the sand, looking for shells.

"We are leaving early tomorrow morning," I said. "Right after breakfast." I was not looking forward to leaving. And I was not looking forward to the long, long car ride home. But I was looking forward to seeing Emily Junior and Hannie and Nancy again.

"We are, too. It takes us almost two hours to get home by plane," Diana said. (She lives in Pennsylvania.)

"You know what? We should write letters to each other," I said.

Diana smiled at me. "That is a great idea. And I have another idea." She leaned over and whispered it in my ear.

"Diana, you are so smart," I said. "Mommy?" I called. "May we go back to the house?"

"Yes," she said. "Be careful climbing the rocks."

"Here is my picture," I said to Diana. I handed her one of my small school pictures. In it I am wearing my pink glasses, and my blue glasses are around my neck. "I wrote 'Love, Karen' on the back."

"Thank you," Diana said. "Here is one of me. I wrote 'Your friend 4-ever' on it."

98

"Thank you." I took her picture and put it in my memory box. That is what Diana's smart idea had been. We were going to make our own memory boxes. We would put them back in the magic garden wall, and hide them again.

Our mommies had cut off tiny locks of our hair, and tied them with new ribbons. We each put in our favorite seashells, and also our woven friendship bracelets. There was one menu from the restaurant we had gone to (where I had tried a clam). We cut it in half, and put the halves in our boxes.

Last, we put in letters we had written to each other.

Mine said:

"Dear Diana,
"This was the best family reunion. I had so much fun with you. Please write to me. And come see me in Stoneybrook. Let's be friends forever. Love, your cousin, Karen."

Then I folded it and wrote SWAK on it
(Sealed With A Kiss). I kissed it and handed
it to her.

Hers said:

"Dear Karen,
"I am so glad we are cousins. We are
twin cousins! One day when I get married, you will be my bridesmaid. See
you next year, I hope! Love, Diana."

Then she folded it and wrote:

2 NICE
2 BE
4 - GOTTEN

on it.
"Thank you," I said. "That is so sweet."
We closed our memory boxes. I hid mine
under the *A* bricks. Diana hid hers under
the *P* bricks. Then we hugged.
"Now, remember," I said. "You cannot
come get the memory boxes without me.
You have to wait, no matter how long."

Diana nodded. "You have to wait, too. We have to do it together. I hope it is next year, at the next family reunion."

"Me, too," I said. "That is so far away. I will be eight then."

"Me, too. Let's make one more wish."

We closed our eyes and made wishes. I think we both wished for the same thing. Can you guess what it was?

With one last look at the magic garden, we walked back to the big house, holding hands.

Saying Good-bye

"Karen, honey, time to wake up," Mommy said softly.

"Ughhhh," I mumbled. I did not want to get up. I did not want to get in the car for a humongously long car ride back to Stoneybrook. I did not want to say good-bye to Diana.

Mommy shook my shoulder. "Last one out of her sleeping bag is a rotten egg," she whispered.

I could not help smiling. I opened my eyes. Diana was in her sleeping bag next

102

to me. We were on the porch. Now that everyone was gone, there were plenty of empty beds upstairs. But we had wanted to spend our last night in Lobster Cove on our porch.

Diana's eyes opened. Mommy smiled at her.

Suddenly Diana leaped out of her sleeping bag and ran for the porch door. "Shake a leg, rotten egg!" she yelled.

I started laughing, and scrambled out of my bag.

Mommy, Seth, Andrew, me, Diana, Kelsey, Aunt Ellen, and Uncle Mark ate one last breakfast at the long dining-room table. I tried to eat slowly, but Seth kept looking at his watch.

"We better hurry, Karen," he said. "The sooner we leave, the sooner we will be back home."

I sighed. Diana sighed, too.

"And we have a plane to catch, Di," said Aunt Ellen.

"I know," Diana said.

The grown-ups got up to finish packing. Andrew went with Kelsey to say good-bye to her frog, Prince Caliber. Andrew loved that frog.

While Mommy and Seth loaded the car, Diana and I sat on the front porch steps. I felt very blue again.

"What if there is no family reunion next year?" I asked sadly.

"What if there is, but I cannot come?" Diana said. "Or you cannot come?"

"Then we cannot open the boxes," I said.

"Maybe we will not open them until we are grown-ups," said Diana.

I wrinkled my nose. "That will be weird. Maybe we will come back here with children of our own."

"And our husbands," Diana said.

"I already have a pretend husband," I told her. "His name is Ricky Torres."

"Wow," said Diana. "I did not know that."

There were so many things we did not

know about each other. We would have to write each other with all the details.

Finally Mommy came to get me. She hugged and kissed Great-aunt Carol, Great-uncle John, and Aunt Ellen and Uncle Mark.

"Please come visit us in Stoneybrook," she said to Aunt Ellen.

"We will try," said Aunt Ellen.

Mommy hugged Kelsey and Diana. Then Andrew hugged everyone. Then I hugged everyone. I saved Diana for last.

"Good-bye," I whispered. I had a lump in my throat. It made it hard to talk.

"Good-bye," Diana whispered back.

Then Mommy took my hand. We walked across the lawn to the stone steps that led down to the driveway. I waved back at Diana. She waved at me.

I swallowed hard.

In the back seat, Andrew and I fastened our seat belts. I did not feel like talking. Mommy and Seth got in the front seats. Mommy was going to drive first. She drove down the driveway and turned onto the road. I looked, but could not see Diana. All I saw was the top of the big house. I saw the attic window.

"Mommy, can I get a frog?" Andrew asked.

"Um, I need to think about it," Mommy said. "Look at all the boats, Karen."

I looked out the window and saw tiny white boats on the ocean. Would I ever see them again?

"I want to eat clams," Andrew said.

Mommy laughed. "Maybe we can eat clams for lunch." She turned the car onto the highway.

Already I missed Diana and the big house and the magic garden and our memory boxes. I thought about the dusty attic. We had found so many neat things in it. There were probably even more things up there that we had not had time to find.

I sat up in my seat. What if . . . what if more of Annemarie's things were up there? I did not know what happened to her after the last diary. Did she ever see Polly again? The next time I went to Lobster Cove, I would look in the attic. Maybe I would find the answers.

But right now, I was going home to Stoneybrook. To my own room and my own bed. And to my two best friends, Hannie and Nancy. I could not wait to tell them about the mystery of the magic garden. And my twin cousin!

"Maybe we can have lunch at a restaurant that has clams for Andrew and other things for me," I said. "Things besides clams."

"That is a very good idea," Mommy said.

"Andrew, do you want to play I Spy?" I asked. We had a long car trip ahead of us. I needed to pass the time.

L. GODWIN

About the Author

ANN M. MARTIN lives in New York City and loves animals, especially cats. She has two cats of her own, Gussie and Woody.

Other books by Ann M. Martin that you might enjoy are *Stage Fright*; *Me and Katie (the Pest)*; and the books in *The Baby-sitters Club* series.

Ann likes ice cream and *I Love Lucy*. And she has her own little sister, whose name is Jane.

Little Sister

Don't miss #77

KAREN'S SCHOOL SURPRISE

"For three points, who can name a planet in our solar system that is surrounded by rings?"

A girl from the other team rang the bell. She was fast!

"Saturn," said the girl.

"That is correct!" replied Mr. Stevens. "Your team now has three points. Here is the next question. How many times does the letter 's' appear in "Mississippi?""

Guess who got the answer right? Me!

"There are four esses in Mississippi," I said.

By the end of the first round, the other team was ahead five points. I was not worried, though. They looked pretty wimpy. And the stunts were still to come.

LITTLE ♦ APPLE®

BABY SITTERS
Little Sister™

by Ann M. Martin,
author of The Baby-sitters Club ®

❑	MQ44300-3	#1	Karen's Witch	$2.95
❑	MQ44259-7	#2	Karen's Roller Skates	$2.95
❑	MQ44299-7	#3	Karen's Worst Day	$2.95
❑	MQ44264-3	#4	Karen's Kittycat Club	$2.95
❑	MQ44258-9	#5	Karen's School Picture	$2.95
❑	MQ44298-8	#6	Karen's Little Sister	$2.95
❑	MQ44257-0	#7	Karen's Birthday	$2.95
❑	MQ42670-2	#8	Karen's Haircut	$2.95
❑	MQ43652-X	#9	Karen's Sleepover	$2.95
❑	MQ43651-1	#10	Karen's Grandmothers	$2.95
❑	MQ43650-3	#11	Karen's Prize	$2.95
❑	MQ43649-X	#12	Karen's Ghost	$2.95
❑	MQ43648-1	#13	Karen's Surprise	$2.95
❑	MQ43646-5	#14	Karen's New Year	$2.95
❑	MQ43645-7	#15	Karen's in Love	$2.95
❑	MQ43644-9	#16	Karen's Goldfish	$2.95
❑	MQ43643-0	#17	Karen's Brothers	$2.95
❑	MQ43642-2	#18	Karen's Home-Run	$2.75
❑	MQ43641-4	#19	Karen's Good-Bye	$2.95
❑	MQ44823-4	#20	Karen's Carnival	$2.95
❑	MQ44824-2	#21	Karen's New Teacher	$2.95
❑	MQ44833-1	#22	Karen's Little Witch	$2.95
❑	MQ44832-3	#23	Karen's Doll	$2.95
❑	MQ44859-5	#24	Karen's School Trip	$2.95
❑	MQ44831-5	#25	Karen's Pen Pal	$2.95
❑	MQ44830-7	#26	Karen's Ducklings	$2.95
❑	MQ44829-3	#27	Karen's Big Joke	$2.95
❑	MQ44828-5	#28	Karen's Tea Party	$2.95
❑	MQ44825-0	#29	Karen's Cartwheel	$2.75
❑	MQ45645-8	#30	Karen's Kittens	$2.95
❑	MQ45646-6	#31	Karen's Bully	$2.95
❑	MQ45647-4	#32	Karen's Pumpkin Patch	$2.95
❑	MQ45648-2	#33	Karen's Secret	$2.95
❑	MQ45650-4	#34	Karen's Snow Day	$2.95
❑	MQ45652-0	#35	Karen's Doll Hospital	$2.95
❑	MQ45651-2	#36	Karen's New Friend	$2.95
❑	MQ45653-9	#37	Karen's Tuba	$2.95
❑	MQ45655-5	#38	Karen's Big Lie	$2.95
❑	MQ45654-7	#39	Karen's Wedding	$2.95
❑	MQ47040-X	#40	Karen's Newspaper	$2.95
❑	MQ47041-8	#41	Karen's School	$2.95
❑	MQ47042-6	#42	Karen's Pizza Party	$2.95
❑	MQ46912-6	#43	Karen's Toothache	$2.95
❑	MQ47043-4	#44	Karen's Big Weekend	$2.95
❑	MQ47044-2	#45	Karen's Twin	$2.95
❑	MQ47045-0	#46	Karen's Baby-sitter	$2.95

More Titles... ➡